Crow Girl

by

Kate Cann

First published in 2005 in Great Britain by
Barrington Stoke Ltd
18 Walker St, Edinburgh EH3 7LP

www.barringtonstoke.co.uk

Reprinted 2007

ISBN: 978-1-84299-346-0

Printed in Great Britain by Bell & Bain Ltd

A Note from the Author

There's nothing magic in this story ... it could happen to you. Crows are clever creatures, and once they get to know you, they'll come to you. I learnt this from an old man in a park, who was being followed by three crows. He told me they waited for him each day by the gate, and he fed them dog biscuits. I was very impressed, and started to feed them too, and watch them.

The story of a lonely teenage girl who could call crows started to form itself in my head. Then my daughter told me about some marvellous black wings that her friend had worn on Halloween night, and the story was made.

Because of the crows, Lily begins to like herself, and become attractive. She starts living, takes risks, grows and is brave.

She fights back. She learns there's no light without the dark.

To Jill –
also a Crow Girl!

Contents

Chapter 1
The Parkway Girls

"Hey – look who it is!" Tanya shouted across the school car park.

"*Lill – eee*!" Jade yelled out.

"*Lill – eee*!!" Jenny and Bella joined in.

"What are *you* doing here, Lily?" Tanya asked. "We thought you'd dropped out."

"Thought you weren't gonna come back," said Jade.

"*I* thought she'd gone to a mental home, didn't you?" Jenny sniggered.

"After all that trouble at the end of last term. Couldn't cope, could you, Lily?" said Bella.

"*Lill – eee*!" they all shouted.

"*Lill – eee*!!"

Lily Stanfield dropped her head further down onto her chest, so that her long, dull brown hair fell over her face. She hunched her back like a turtle. Then she kept on walking past the Parkway Girls. All four of them were leaning against the wall of the gym. As they watched Lily walk past, they sneered at her and sniggered. They knew there'd be no comeback.

The start of the new autumn term was always horrible, but this one was even worse. Last summer term had been really bad. Lily had spent a lot of time off school. She'd said she had stomach pains, pains so bad she couldn't do anything. She just sat with her arms wrapped round her middle. Her mum

2

had made her go to the doctor but he couldn't find anything wrong. In the end, Lily's mum got it out of her that the Parkway Girls were the reason she was hiding at home. Her mum was very upset. She went to talk to Mr Thomas, the head teacher. There'd been meetings with other teachers and lots of talking. Everything was "looked into". At last Mr Thomas asked Lily's mum to come back in to school so he could tell her what the plan was.

"I wouldn't call it bullying," Mr Thomas had said. "Not *real* bullying. I agree the Parkway Girls have been a bit loud, a bit unthinking maybe, but Lily – well, she's a very sensitive girl, isn't she?"

"So you're not even going to get those horrible girls in here?" Lily's mum said. She was angry. "You're not even going to talk to them?"

"I'm not sure that would be a good idea," Mr Thomas replied. He looked at Lily's mum and frowned. "You see – I don't want to make a big deal of it. In the long run ... that might make things worse for Lily, and we don't want that, do we? Lily takes things to heart too much. She gets upset too easily. Best thing all round would be to forget it, have a good rest over the summer holidays, and make a fresh start next term."

In a way, of course, Mr Thomas was right. Maybe Lily did get upset too easily. But it wasn't just the Parkway Girls that upset her.

It was everyone. There were the boys who laughed at her and teased her or just didn't see her at all. Then there was Sonia Smith. Sonia was the most gorgeous girl in the whole year. She and her group of clone-friends were always making sly remarks about how Lily looked.

Sonia walked past Lily now. She muttered something to Mattie who was one of her adoring clones.

"I *know!*" Mattie squealed back. "She's like a big blob with four strings attached!"

Lily hunched her shoulders higher and tucked her chin in to hide the hurt. She was longing to cry as she went on into the classroom.

Chapter 2
The Crow

Lily hardly spoke to anyone all day. Even Marsha Hill, who used to have a bit of time for her, seemed to be keeping out of Lily's way. At long last, the school day came to an end, and Lily could escape.

To comfort herself, she went into a sweet shop. She didn't go into the shop right by the school, where people would jeer at her for buying sweets. She chose a sweet shop that was half way home and bought a giant Kit Kat. Then she took the shortcut home that went past the edge of the Wakeless Woods.

Biting into the Kit Kat was the first truly good thing that had happened to Lily all day. The sugar in it made her feel better at once. As she chewed and swallowed, she felt her spirits lift. She knew that feeling wouldn't last, but it was so lovely while it lasted. She started to lick the chocolate off the end of the Kit Kat, slowly, to make it last longer.

The woods were looking their best. Vines and ivy grew over the rubbish that people had dumped on the edge of the woods. The low autumn sun glowed through the branches of the trees and lit up the red and orange berries that hung there.

Lily didn't know why, but she left the little lane she always took on the way home. Instead of going past the garden gates of the endless row of houses at the edge of the woods, she went deeper into the woods. She followed the new path until it came to a stop, in a small clearing in the trees.

A single crow was hunched on a branch, looking at her. Lily flapped her hand at it to shoo it away, but it didn't move. "What's the matter? Are you hungry?" she asked.

The crow stared back at her without blinking.

"What's wrong with all these berries? Why don't you eat those? They too healthy for you?"

The crow stared back at her, still not blinking. "You're like me, aren't you? A Junk Food Queen." Lily broke off the bit of Kit Kat where she'd licked away the chocolate, and tossed it towards the crow. The crow lifted silently off the branch and floated down on wide black wings to the ground. It found the bit of biscuit, pecked it up, and looked up at Lily again.

"That's your lot, mate," she said. Then she turned round and started to walk back through the trees.

A sudden whoosh of wings overhead made her duck. The crow flew over her head, and landed on a branch just ahead of her. Then it fixed its beady eyes on her again, with its huge black beak pointing straight at her.

Lily broke off another bit of her Kit Kat. She tossed it on the narrow path in front of her. The crow flapped down, pecked it up, and flew back to the branch.

Lily walked on, and heard the rush of wings again, right behind her. The crow was following her. It was pretty scary. It was playing leapfrog with her. Whenever Lily walked on, the crow flew over her head, and then landed on a branch just ahead of her.

"Last bit!" Lily said in a loud, strict voice to make herself feel in control of things. She threw the last chunk of Kit Kat up into the air.

The crow tumbled down from the branch like an acrobat. It caught the Kit Kat as it

was falling. Then it landed on a branch above
Lily's head. It stretched out its neck and
fixed its eyes on her.

Lily was really spooked. She started to
run, and as she ran she sang loudly and
waved her arms about to frighten off the
crow. Only when she got to the lane at the
edge of the woods did she feel safe again.

Chapter 3

One Big Blob

The big kitchen in Lily's house always seemed to be full of loud, active ten-year-old boys. Lily had twin ten-year-old brothers, and Lily's mum had worked out that, if the twins were going to get invited anywhere, then she had to invite their friends back. A *lot.*

But today Lily was lucky. The big kitchen was empty, and Lily's mum was waiting with a plate of oozing jam doughnuts and the teapot all ready to fill. "How did it go, dear?" she asked, her voice worried, as soon as Lily walked in.

"Oh – you know," muttered Lily. "OK."

"Did those horrible girls start on you again?" Lily's mum poured boiling water into the teapot. Then she turned round and gave her daughter a big smile as if *she* could make everything all right.

"Well – they shouted out a few things when I walked into school. About me being off last term and everything. But I ignored them—"

"Well done – that's the way!"

"—and they left me alone after that."

"So it was OK, then?"

Lily thought of the silence of the day, no-one talking to her, no-one seeing her. "Yeah, it was OK," she mumbled.

"And how's that nice girl Marsha?"

"She's ... she's fine."

"You'll have to ask her back one day soon. I'll tell you when the twins are going to be out, eh?" Then Lily's mum pushed the plate of doughnuts towards her daughter. Lily remembered about the Kit Kat and she knew she should say no. Then she thought – *my first day at school's been so bad I can't even tell Mum about it*, and so she put out her hand, and took the fattest doughnut she could see.

Upstairs in her room, Lily stripped off her school uniform and dumped it on her chair. With just her bra and pants on, she turned round to look at herself in the full-length mirror on the wall. What was it that cow Mattie had said? That she was a big blob with four strings stuck on the corners. She stood and looked hard at her thin arms and legs. Her breasts and middle were all wrong. They didn't go with her arms and legs at all. She hated her large breasts. They were just like more rolls of fat, rolling down to meet the rolls of fat around her middle. Mattie was right. She was just one big blob.

Lily grabbed a baggy sweatshirt and jeans and put them on quickly. This was her out-of-school uniform. These days that was all she wore. Before all the trouble at school she'd dressed a bit Goth. She didn't wear anything to make her stand out, just long black skirts and silver chains and stuff – but she'd loved it. Then even that had got her teased. "Lill-eee thinks she looks thin in black!" the Parkway Girls had sneered, when they saw her in town. "It'll take more than black to do that, darlin'!"

That night Lily had a dream about the crow from the Wakeless Woods. She was standing, watching it and it flew in circles over the Parkway Girls. The crow was cawing and screeching, and they were terrified. Tanya, the leader of the Parkway Girls ran away, but the crow followed her, flying from branch to branch.

14

Then it swooped down on her face, stabbing with its beak.

Lily woke up the next morning, with her head full of the dream about the crow. *There's something in me that's like the crow*, she thought. *That's why I dreamt about it. I'm going back to the woods tonight, to see if it's there.*

After she'd had her breakfast, Lily went to the fridge. She knew birds liked fat, so she got out some cheese, cut off a big lump, wrapped it up in tin foil and slipped it into her pocket.

The school day passed much as yesterday had done. No-one spoke to her at all except when one of Sonia's clones told her to shift because she was blocking the corridor.

As soon as school finished, Lily went to the woods. She turned onto the path that led her to the clearing in the trees. But she couldn't see the crow anywhere. She walked all round the clearing – it was almost a complete circle. *I bet witches meet up here*, she thought. She was enjoying making herself feel scared. A little path that she hadn't seen yesterday led out of the clearing on the other side. Lily hesitated for a moment and then stepped on to it.

This path was even narrower than the other one. Branches hung right down overhead, and she had to push them aside. The late sun slanted though the trees and made the shadows look darker. *This is stupid*, she thought. *I could get lost. Mugged, raped. No-one comes here on their own. No-one.*

Suddenly, she froze. She'd heard a rustling noise, right near her. Her eyes swivelled round. She scanned the bushes and brambles on both sides of the path. Something was moving, something hunched and dark, low on the ground. Lily's heart thudded. She could hear breathing. It was coming closer.

Chapter 4

Deep in the Woods

There was a sound of cracking twigs, and the bushes split apart –

And a little black spaniel bustled onto the path and ran up to Lily, barking and wagging its tail.

"Didi!" called a woman's voice. "Here!"

Then the woman walked up. She was old but she looked full of life. "Evening!" she said to Lily.

"Hello!" Lily squawked. She bent down to pat the spaniel, trying to cover up how scared she'd been.

"Oh, Didi – you like a fuss, don't you?" said the woman as she patted and stroked the spaniel. Then she turned to Lily. "Where's your dog, dear?" she asked.

Lily didn't feel she could say she was just out for a walk on her own. "He's run on ahead," she mumbled.

"Bless him! They do like these woods, don't they? Haven't seen you here before."

"I ... er, no," mumbled Lily. "Mum ... she thinks it's not safe."

"Oh – that sounds just like my son!" the woman said with a snort. "He tells me not to come here on my own. But I tell him, I feel a lot safer here than I do in the centre of town! Anyway – must get on, dear. See you again, I expect."

And she walked on. Lily felt a rush of relief and good feeling now she wasn't scared any more. She went on, deeper into the woods. *I had no idea the trees went on this far*, she thought. *They're huge!* After a while, she came to a second clearing. It was bigger than the first and the shape of an oval. Lily thought it was more beautiful somehow. A large tree had fallen down in the middle of the clearing and it was lit by the low sun. Sitting on the tree trunk, as if it was waiting for her, was the crow.

Lily could swear it was the same one. It had a flash of white on its neck – she'd noticed that yesterday.

"Hi!" she shouted out. "Want a bit of cheese?"

She took the tinfoil packet out of her pocket, broke off a lump of cheese, and tossed it to the crow. As it flew down to pick it up, there was a swish of wings overhead, and another crow flew into the clearing – then another. Lily felt a thrill of fear. Then she laughed, broke off two more bits of cheese and threw them. She sat down on the tree trunk and soon there were five crows all around her. They stabbed at the grass with their great black beaks.

On the way back home, two of the crows followed her – White-flash and another one with a ragged wing. As she tossed down the last of the cheese, they swooped down for it, then flapped past her and waited on the branches ahead for her to catch up.

When Lily got home, her mother was standing in the open front door. "Everything all right, love?" she asked. "You're so late!" Lily could tell she was afraid she'd got into some trouble at going-home time. That she thought Lily had been bullied by the Parkway Girls or something.

"I'm fine!" Lily replied. "I just hung out for a bit, after school. With Marsha, and everyone."

Lily's mum smiled as if, all at once, the sun had come out in her face. She beamed at Lily and said, "How *lovely!* Well come on in … dinner's ready!"

Suddenly Lily felt starving. Dinner was pizza, with salad. The twins didn't want the salad, so Lily finished it all off.

The radio was on in the kitchen as Lily helped clear up. She heard a man talking about how clever some animals and birds are. He had just said something about crows. He was saying how they'd done some tests on different birds and animals, and crows came out top. They were even cleverer than chimps. Chimps could use tools – but crows *made* them. Lily stopped stacking the dishwasher to listen to how a female crow had made a bit of wire into a hook so that she could pull a tiny bucket of food out of a hole in the ground.

This is a sign, Lily said to herself. *It's someone, somewhere* ... telling me *something.*

She looked up *crow* on the Internet. There was an amazing set of poems by Ted Hughes, a funky gothic film, and some old Celtic myths. They told of war goddesses who turned into crows to warn of death in battle. Then there was lots of info about real crows, how clever they were, how they could be trained.

Over the next few weeks, Lily started going to the Wakeless Woods every day after school.

When she thought about the crows and being with them, she didn't feel so bad about the loneliness and misery of school each day. She'd go straight to the oval-shaped clearing with a bag of scraps – bacon rinds, meat fat, cheese – and feed them. She loved the long walk in the woods, and she loved the crows as they floated down to her like large black crosses. She still felt a slight thrill of fear as they swooped down to her, and she loved that too.

Three crows were always there – White-flash, Ragwing and the biggest crow, the one Lily called the Morrigan, after a Celtic goddess. Sometimes as many as seven came for Lily's scraps. As soon as she entered the woods, the crows would gather round her, cawing. Then they'd escort her to the clearing. If the crows weren't there when Lily arrived, she'd call *kaaa-kaaa-kaaaa*, copying their own harsh cries. They'd fly to meet her with their claws tucked underneath them like a plane's landing wheels.

Lily was training them. They'd sit on branches, and she'd toss a scrap to each crow in turn, and it would fly down to catch it in mid-air. They'd all wait their turn. Even the Morrigan waited. She normally chased the other ones off when there was food about but she seemed to understand that this was different.

If Lily held up both arms together it was a sign that she was going to throw a lot of food, so they'd all fly down together. They flew in low circles around Lily, which was terrifying but wonderful too.

Afterwards, they'd perch beside her on the fallen tree trunk, and keep her company. Then they'd always escort her out of the woods again.

Going to the woods made Lily feel so good that more and more she forgot to stop and buy chocolate after school. And, she was getting home late too, just in time for dinner. She was always hungry and she'd eat all the vegetables the twins wouldn't eat.

Lily wasn't aware of it, but walking in the woods and the change of diet were making her look a lot better.

Chapter 5

Changes

At the start of October, Mum told Lily it really was time she went to visit her grandmother. "Grandy was on the phone to me the other day," said Mum. "And she was asking about her favourite granddaughter."

"Mum – I'm her *only* granddaughter!"

"That's why she loves you so much! Come on, Lily. This Saturday. Or it'll be Christmas before we know it."

So that Saturday at 11 o'clock, Lily set off on the 50-minute bus journey (one change) to go and have lunch with Grandy. Grandy was Dad's mother, and she was called Grandy because she was rather posh and grand compared to Lily's other grandma.

Lily felt sad as she juddered along on the bus. When she was little, Lily had visited Grandy all the time. But when her happy little Lily turned into a lumpy teenager with no energy, Grandy found it hard to hide her feelings. And Lily had come to dread the way Grandy looked at her nowadays – as if Lily was a big let-down.

The lunch went well. Grandy had cooked salmon, mashed potato and green beans, and she didn't ask Lily too many questions. Instead Grandy chatted about her friends and her charity work. They were clearing the table when Grandy suddenly put her hands on Lily's shoulders, and gave her an enormous smile. "You're looking better, dear," she said. "It was just what I told your mother. You were in what I call 'the ugly duckling phase'!

I can say that to you now that you're coming out of it."

"I don't feel like I am," muttered Lily, "not really."

"Oh, but you are. You look slimmer, your skin is better. Now ..." Grandy dropped her hands from Lily's shoulders. "Do something for me, dear. Lace your fingers together, in front of you. That's right. Now push your hands away from you, as far as they'll go. Good. Now raise your arms, high up above your head – higher, further back! *Strre ... e ... etch!* Excellent. Now here. Look."

And she turned Lily to face the long gold mirror above the fireplace.

Lily looked at herself, all stretched out. "See?" said Grandy, and she laughed out loud. "You've got a waist! You look wonderful!"

Lily couldn't help smiling. "I wish I could walk around like this!" she said.

"But you can, dear. Bring your arms down slowly. That's it. Relax your hands by your sides. But don't collapse. Pretend there's a string, coming out of the top of your head, and an angel is hanging down from a cloud and holding it up!"

"*Wha ... aat?*" laughed Lily.

"Never mind – just hold your stomach in, that's right. Now walk – walk across the room."

Lily turned and glided across the room, as if she could feel the string on her head. Grandy burst out clapping. "Posture, you see, dear?" she said with delight. "That's what we called it in my day. Now fetch me my handbag. We're going out."

Forty minutes later, Grandy and Lily were arguing in quiet, fierce voices in the lingerie department of the smart, old-style department store at the end of the high street. "I am *not* getting *measured*!" Lily was hissing. "No way!"

"Lily, *darling*! If your mother wasn't always so busy with the twins, she would have explained to you by now that it's *most important* to be measured properly for a *bra*!"

"I'm not undressing in front of—" Lily broke off. A motherly looking woman who was much bigger than Lily was standing in front of her with a tape measure. "After a new bra, are we dear?" she asked. She whisked Lily away into a small changing room with a big mirror.

Lily shut her eyes, she was so embarrassed. But she did what the woman asked. She took her top off, then her tatty old bra, and held up her arms so that the woman could slide a tape measure round her ... and then it was all over. The shop assistant was saying, "Thirty-six D – lovely!

Lucky you! I recommend underwired, for that size. Shall I bring you some bras to try on?"

Fifteen minutes later, Lily was looking at her reflection in the changing-room mirror. She couldn't believe what she could see. All the bras she'd tried on had been great, but this one was perfect. All her old bulges had vanished. She didn't wobble when she moved. She was comfortable. And she looked *fantastic*.

"That's the one!" said Grandy, firmly. "We'll take two, please. In white."

"Would you mind, Grandy," breathed Lily, fast, "if we made that one white and one *black*?"

Chapter 6

Night Woods

As soon as she got home, Lily pulled open her wardrobe and dug around at the bottom for a black, gothic-style dress she'd hurled there a few months ago. She'd been feeling desperate and thought she'd never wear that dress again. But now she found it, stripped off her jeans and T-shirt, and pulled it on. Then she stood up tall, like Grandy had told her to. She turned to face the mirror, and held in her stomach.

The dress was still a bit tight, but somehow it was *good* tight now. It clung to her hips, then flared out. It had a low neckline that looked wonderful with her new black bra. She loved the long, cobwebby sleeves, and the jagged, zigzag hem.

She pulled on the high-heeled boots she'd bought to go with the dress, and turned to the mirror again. She brushed her long brown hair back from her face. Then she put on some black eyeliner. Her hand was trembling with excitement. After that she found some mascara, and red lipstick. She looked so good now, it scared her. She knew she'd never dare go out looking like this. Outside, in just a couple of hours' time, Saturday night would be in full swing, and once again she'd be left out of it. She'd be stuck at home watching the telly while everyone else *lived* ...

But it was a warm evening and it wouldn't be dark for an hour or so. Lily ran from her room, down to the kitchen. She grabbed some oatmeal biscuits as she went. Then she raced towards the Wakeless Woods.

Even if she was too scared to let anyone else see her, *the crows* could see her. They gathered round her, cawing. "Well?" she called out, "What d'you reckon?" When they got to the clearing Lily held up both arms together and her long cobwebby sleeves billowed out. She threw the bits of biscuit in the air and the crows flapped round her in circles. She laughed out loud in sheer delight. She felt like a witch who could summon crows by magic. She felt like the Morrigan with her sisters flying round her.

It was dark when Lily got back onto the lane behind the houses. Suddenly she made up her mind not to go home just yet. Instead she headed into town. She made herself walk tall. She strode out on her high-heeled boots. She pretended she was heading to a party. People looked at her, but only the way everyone checks out everyone on a Saturday night. A gang of boys catcalled and shouted, "Where you off to, darling?" She walked around for over an hour, just enjoying being part of it all. Then she went home again, alone.

When Monday morning came round, Lily put on her new white bra to go to school. She brushed her hair just a bit back from her face. She walked tall into school, but as soon as she saw the Parkway Girls she rounded her shoulders like a turtle again. She didn't want them to notice her.

Chapter 7
Razzle Dazzle

There were only three weeks to go till Halloween. Lily *loved* Halloween. She loved the way the dark side came out to play, she loved the witches and skeletons you saw in all the shops. A few times, Lily took a longer route home from school so she could visit a joke and costume shop called *Razzle Dazzle.* This shop came to life at Halloween. There were grisly masks and tricks and toys crammed in its windows and on its shelves. A black fishing net hung at the back of the shop to make a bat-infested cave and that was where the Halloween costumes were. This year, among the zombies and vampires, there was something special on show – a fantastic pair of black wings. Dark angel wings.

Crow wings.

Lily couldn't stop looking at them. She wanted them so badly it hurt. But a large label attached to them said *£75*. Who could afford that? Not Lily.

Even so, she couldn't keep away from them. While the shop was busy she edged up close to them, past the sign that said *Do not touch.* She wanted to inspect them properly. The feathers were fake, but so good they looked real. The shopkeeper came up to show a rich-looking customer how they worked. Lily watched. There was a bar between the wings. When you pulled a short string, the bar folded up and closed the wings. If you let go of the string, the wings would open again.

They were so simple, and yet they looked like if you put them on, you could fly.

On 13th October, Lily was sitting eating lunch at school, on her own as usual. The next moment Marsha came over, dumped her tray down on the same table and said, "Can I join you, Lill?"

Lily looked up quickly, then went on looking at the plate in front of her. She wanted to talk to Marsha, of course she did, but she was hurt by the way Marsha had dropped her before. Marsha pulled out a chair, thumped down on it, and squawked, "Lill – what is it? Why've you got the hump?"

Lily shrugged. She didn't trust herself to answer. "You've been avoiding me since the start of term!" Marsha went on. As she said it, she believed it, but the truth was that Marsha had been the one avoiding Lily. Misery had surrounded Lily like a bad smell, and Marsha had been repelled by it.

But over the last few weeks, Lily had changed. It wasn't just that she looked better, somehow she wasn't so sad and needy any more. Marsha felt like she could talk to her again.

"I haven't been avoiding you," muttered Lily. "I thought you were avoiding me!"

"No!" said Marsha, warmly, "'course I wasn't! Anyway, we've caught up together now. Hey, have you heard what happened between Sally and Max?"

"No?"

"He snatched her phone away while she was texting Rory Parsons, and read it, and it was this really sexy stuff! He went *mad*!"

"I bet! What happened?"

"He dumped her! He was really yelling at her, she was well upset ..."

Lily sat and listened happily to Marsha's gossip as the girls ate their lunch. They were still nattering as the bell went to start afternoon school. "You gotta come out with us sometime!" Marsha said, as they both stood up to go. "Hey – you going to Kyle's Halloween party?"

"I thought he wasn't having one this year?" said Lily.

"Oh, he just said that so we'd tell him he had to! He was moaning on about how his mum was doing up the house for Halloween anyway, saying she liked it better than Christmas. So we nagged him and made him change his mind about the party! I mean – come *on!* If your mum *wants* you to have a party, you gotta say yes, haven't you?"

"Yeah," said Lily. "You have!"

"So, you coming?"

"Well – he hasn't asked me yet ..."

"Lill – *eee!* He's not gonna hand out little invites with pumpkins on, like when we were 12, is he? 'Course you can come. Halloween's on a Saturday this year, it's great. Come with us lot, it'll be fine!" And Marsha waved happily, and spun off towards the dining room exit.

All that afternoon, Lily could think of nothing else but Kyle Hooper's Halloween Party. Kyle was one of the school stars, everyone knew that. He was tall, and not exactly fit-looking, but he was funny, and confident. He was cool enough to carry off having Halloween parties every year. Cool enough to get away with telling people they had to dress up for them.

And now Lily was going to go to the next one.

She thought of her gothic dress, the way it had looked so good with her high-heeled boots and new black bra. What a great basis for a Halloween costume it would be! She thought of the way she'd look so different with eye make-up and lipstick on, and how she could walk tall like Grandy had shown her. She thought of how she didn't dare show this new look to the Parkway Girls, how she couldn't bring herself to look too different at school.

She thought that the Parkway Girls would be sure to be at the party – Kyle thought they were "good value".

She thought of the dark angel wings in *Razzle Dazzle*.

Bit by bit, like paint colours blurring into each other, all her thoughts came together. *I could make the party the start of the new me,* she told herself. *I could make a costume that was so stunning everyone would notice me. And after that, I couldn't go back to hiding. I'd dress different, walk different,* be *different ...*

Her mind made another leap. Kyle's house was one of the houses that backed onto the lane behind the Wakeless Woods. White-flash, Ragwing and the Morrigan sometimes flew with her a little way along it, when she was on the way home. She could ... oh, God, she *could*.

A great shudder ran through her.

Lily was thinking things that scared her and made her feel great, all at the same time.

Chapter 8
The Wings

The next day after school, Lily rushed along to *Razzle Dazzle*. She prayed that the wings would still be there. To her relief they were still there – they'd been moved to the front of the shop and strapped to a cheap-looking dummy wearing a skeleton mask. Lily could look at the wings even more closely now, and she looked at them for a long time and tried to remember every detail.

Her plan was to start making a pair just like them tonight.

Outside the shop, she pulled a sketchbook from her bag and drew the wings. She jotted down everything she could remember about the string and the bar between the wings. She looked at how the feathers were all fixed onto the wire frame. Then she went into a hardware store and bought a good long length of strong, thick wire, and a spool of thin wire. Next, she went to the pet shop and bought some dog biscuits shaped like little bones. She knew the crows would love these because they had fat in them. After all this, she hurried along to the Wakeless Woods. "Mustn't neglect my babies, must I?" she muttered to herself, as she sped along through the trees. "Not now they're part of my master plan ..."

It got dark earlier now that it was mid-October, and it was dusk already. Lily could just about make out the hunched shape of the crows in the oval-shaped clearing. She called *kaa-kaaa-kaaaa*, and they floated down towards her like black ghosts. She broke three bone-biscuits up and tossed the pieces in the air and the crows caught them, or followed them to the ground. Then she turned to go. As she'd hoped, White-flash, Ragwing and the Morrigan flew after her. There were two other crows as well but the Morrigan chased them away with a harsh *kraaaaw!*

Every few minutes Lily stopped to toss up bits of broken biscuit. That way she made sure the three crows followed her right to the edge of the woods. When they got to the lane behind the row of houses, Lily threw the biscuit bits more often. The crows followed her but she could tell they were getting more nervous as they got closer and closer to the houses. They reached a bright strip of light that shone out from a garden shed. The crows refused to cross it. They flapped into the air, and flew back into the dark trees.

Lily wasn't upset. She walked on. Kyle Hooper's garden gate was only a few metres away. Once the crows understood the light wasn't going to hurt them, they'd follow her further. They'd follow her all the way if she had some really tasty bits of bacon fat to throw to them.

Lily grinned to herself, and hurried on. She was going to do it. She was going to train the crows to follow her all the way along the lane, to the bottom of Kyle Hooper's garden.

And then, on Halloween night, she was going to arrive at the party all winged and stunning, as mistress of the crows, as the Morrigan, as *Crow Girl*!

Chapter 9
Halloween Plans

Making her wings was a lot, lot harder
than Lily had thought it would be. The frame
and the bar and string were OK. It was the
feathers that were a problem. She started by
collecting real feathers, but she couldn't find
many that were black. So she collected
white-grey pigeon feathers from the park and
dyed them with ink. Even so, she didn't have
enough to go round the outside of the frame,
let alone fill it. She tried to make feathers
from cardboard, and then from black crepe
paper, but they looked rubbish and nothing
like the ones on the wings in *Razzle Dazzle*.

Would the wings ever turn out right? Lily had a few horrible bleak days when nothing she did worked. She began to think she'd never have the nerve to walk into the party all dressed up anyway. If she did, everyone would laugh at her, and the Parkway Girls would go on about how sad she was for putting all that effort in just to look like a prat ...

But then she hit on the idea of using black bin bags. She cut out jagged feather shapes and stapled them onto the wire frame. They looked great – limp and shiny and sinister. She put the few real feathers she had around the tips and the top of the frame. Slowly, the wings took shape. They weren't perfect, she thought, as she stapled the last few feathers onto the frame, but it didn't matter. After all, no-one was going to see them from close up.

Lily sat back on her heels. *No-one was going to see them from close up?* Where had that thought come from?

She had the wings, she had the dress and her boots. All she needed now was to do her face and hair. Lily didn't need anyone else to do a makeover on her, like in teen sitcoms. She knew just what to do. She bought some dramatic make-up that was great for Halloween but made her look gorgeous, too. She bought glossy dark purple hair dye to make her dull brown hair the colour of a crow's wings. She was going to dye her hair on the morning of Halloween. Then she would toss her hair back from her face instead of letting it hang over her eyes like drab curtains.

She tried her wonderful black bra on again, and this time she made the straps a bit shorter. For the first time in her life she had a cleavage!

In the secrecy of her room, Lily tried putting on the make-up, and the dress and the wings. She couldn't believe what the mirror showed her. She stood tall, like Grandy had said, and remembered about the angel leaning down from a cloud, holding the string on her head and pulling her up tall. It was a dark angel with black wings just like hers. The angel was laughing because the Parkway Girls had just come in and were stunned at how fantastic Lily was looking.

Lily went on training the three crows. Now they were brave enough to cross the strip of light from the garden shed. They followed her all the way to Kyle Hooper's garden gate.

She also practised her crow screams. *Kraaaaw! Kraaaaw!*

Three days to go till Halloween.

Chapter 10
Halloween Night

8 o'clock, Halloween night. Lily stood in the oval clearing in the Wakeless Woods. She was wearing her Goth dress and high-heeled boots, with her eyes made up huge and beautiful. The crow-wings were strapped to her back. They were fixed in the shut position and they felt so light and right on her back. She threw her newly-black, glossy hair away from her face, and thought she'd never felt more scared in her life. This was *risk.* The dark angel of risk. If her careful, daring plan went wrong, it would be awful, worse than awful, it would be death ...

But if it went *right* ...

Lily pulled some bacon rind from the large bag of scraps she'd brought. Then she lifted her arms, and her long, cobwebby sleeves spun out. "*Kaa-kaaa-kaaaa!!*" she called out. The crows were roosting up in the tree branches. They wanted to be left alone, but when she called out again they floated down and swooped on the rinds she threw.

Right away, she set off back down the narrow path through the trees. The only light was from the moon, but it was enough. White-flash, Ragwing and the Morrigan flew after her, greedy now for the scraps she tossed back over her shoulder.

At the edge of the wood, Lily started walking slowly along the lane behind the row of houses. The crows followed her. Together, they arrived at the gate at the end of Kyle's long, overgrown garden.

This was it.

She opened the rickety gate and slipped inside. Her closed wings brushed past low branches. The moon was behind clouds now, and it was very dark where she stood. Lily tossed a few more strips of bacon rind on to the grass in front of her, and the crows flapped past her and straight down to seize them. Then they flew up to the low branches of the trees at the end of the garden, waiting for more.

Perfect. Lily looked towards the house. A string of fairy lights shaped like little skulls glittered on a bush, three pumpkins hung from trees and glowed orange. There were no lights on in the house, only candles. Lily could see dark shapes moving about in the kitchen and heard loud music and laughing. *Time to get everyone's attention*, she thought, and opened her mouth to scream out crow noises.

Silence. She couldn't force herself to make a sound. She felt like she was going to be sick. She felt like a total fool. *I can't do this, I can't carry this off. What are they gonna think? That I've tried too hard, I'm pathetic, I tried and messed up, I'm sad ...*

Then she thought of the hours and hours she'd put in, making the wings, planning all this ... *are you just gonna waste all that?* She felt angry at herself. *This was going to be the start of the new you! Go on – do it!*

A group of kids had come out onto the decking at the top of the garden. Some of them were lighting up cigarettes. They looked bored. *Now!* Lily told herself, but she still couldn't make a sound.

Then suddenly, the clouds scudded away in front of the moon. Moonlight slanted down like a spotlight right in front of her.

And Lily thought, *It's Halloween!* She took a deep breath, and shrieked into the night.

Chapter 11
Terror!

"Can you hear *that*?" one of the kids on the decking shouted.

"What the hell is it?" said another.

"It's coming from down there, the bottom of the garden ..."

"Joe, is that you pissing about down there?"

"It's weird, it's like a bird ..."

"Turn the music down! Hey – you lot – *turn the music down!* There's someone down there!"

Lily shrieked out one last "*Kraawww!*" and watched – her heart hammering. More people came out from the house and the group on the decking got bigger. A few people started moving down the garden towards her. Everyone was laughing, excited, playing at being scared. "You go first!" shouted a girl, and pushed Kyle towards Lily.

Lily's heart lurched. Kyle was pointing straight at her. "Who the hell are you?" he shouted, "Come on out of there!"

And Lily stepped forward, half into the pool of moonlight, a dark shadow across her face. She let go of the string on her wings and felt them creak open. They lifted slow and perfect, they spread full and wide and terrifying.

And the group gasped, backing away from her. "What the *hell* is that?"

"OK – who is it?" shouted Kyle again. "Stop messing about!"

"It's got wings. No-one here had wings!"

"Jesus, *who is it?*"

The corners of Lily's mouth slid upwards. Her plan was working! The feeling of success pulsed through her, sweet and steady. She pulled on the string to make the wings close, and then opened them again. She took another step forward, towards the group. Everyone started to stumble back, pushing against each other in panic, trying to get away. Then one of the boys stopped. "Oh, for *Christ's* sake," he roared, "let's *rush it*!"

A few of the boys lurched towards her. As they did, Lily scooped the last of the bacon rind out of her bag. She put some in both of her hands, and threw her arms in the air like she was cursing everyone. "*Kaa-kaaa-kaaaa!!*" she shrieked. The crows lifted off the branches, and she flung the rind at the boys.

The three crows swooped down, in a rush and blur of beaks and claws. Ragwing caught a scrap in mid-air and flew over the heads below. White-flash and the Morrigan screeched as they headed to the ground, their wings beating in the faces of Kyle and his terrified friends.

Tanya, the leader of the Parkway Girls, was the first to run. With a howl, she turned on her heels and sped towards the house. Her friend Jade followed her. Bella and Jenny were close behind. Lily saw the gorgeous Sonia Smith scream and run back inside. Then, as one, the whole group fled.

It was perfect, it was beyond perfect. Lily ducked back into the shadow, then slipped out of the open gate. She could still hear screaming and shouting.

"Come on, let's look for it!" Kyle shouted.

"*I'm* not bloody going down there again!" someone shouted back.

"It's vanished!"

"Who the *hell* was it?"

"Come on, stop being such a pussy!"

"OK, *you* go if you're so brave!"

Lily grinned as she untied the wings, slipped them off, and pushed them under a bush at the other side of the lane. She hadn't planned to do this, but suddenly it seemed right. She didn't want anyone to know how she'd done it – she wanted it to be a mystery. Three shapes flew round her as she hid the wings under the bushes. "Thank you *so much*, darlings!" she whispered, and the crows flapped back into the woods to roost.

Then Lily stood up tall, smoothed her dress down, and went back in through the rickety garden gate.

Chapter 12
Bliss!

Kyle began to lead the group back down the garden again. Then he suddenly shouted, "Oh, holy *shit*, it's back!"

One of the boys had fetched a torch from the house, and shone it straight at her face.

"Oh, my God – it's Lily!"

"It's Lily Stanfield!"

"Yeah, it's me!" Lily said, loud, as she moved forward. "What's the problem? I was invited, wasn't I?"

Kyle got hold of her arm. "That was *amazing*!" he breathed. "How d'you do it?"

"Do what?" she asked. She felt wonderful. She felt like she was shining, lighting up the night.

"You know – the wings!" insisted Kyle. "The birds! There was one big bird, and three flying ones ..."

Lily smiled. "What've you been drinking, Kyle?"

Several people laughed – Kyle joined in, not taking his eyes off her. It seemed like the whole party had surged out into the garden. There were people all around her. She heard, "Oh, this is *so cool*." She heard, "Jesus, I was so *scared*. How'd she do it?" And from Tom Morris she heard, "Never mind the wings, look at her *tits*!"

Marsha was at her side, all possessive of her friend. "How d'you do it, Lill? Come on – you gotta tell *me*!"

61

"Yeah, Lily – stop pissing about!" grinned Kyle. "We wanna know how you did it!"

Lily lifted her arms again, and her long sleeves billowed. "You look fantastic!" gasped Mattie.

"D'you see any wings?" Lily asked, sweetly. "Maybe it was these you saw."

Uproar from the crowd. "We know what we saw!"

"Anyway, apart from you there were these three massive *birds*—" Tom Morris said.

"Or they coulda been bats ..." added Kyle.

"Or flying imps, or something ..."

"Crows, they were *crows*!"

"You had huge *wings*—" Kyle put in.

"And a *beak*!"

"Oh come on," laughed Lily, "you saying I *changed*? You saying I ... *shape-shifted*? *Skin-turned*?"

They were words she'd learnt from the Celtic myths she'd read about crows. As she said them now they sounded like a witch's spell. "*Woo ... oow*," breathed Tom Morris, full of admiration.

"She changed like Spider Man!" someone yelped.

"Yeah! Bird Girl!"

"*Crow* Girl!"

"*Crow Girl*!"

"God, this is so *cool*!" laughed Kyle. "I thought this party was gonna be a drag and it's *so cool!* Hey, Lily – you coming inside? You wanna drink?"

For the rest of the party, everyone paid Lily more attention than she could handle.

Everyone had a different idea about Crow Girl. Some kids said it was all some kind of trick, from a PowerPoint projector maybe. Lily just smiled and pretended not to know what they were on about. She whispered to Marsha that she'd "explain later", and after that Marsha had a smug smile for the rest of the party and kept telling people *she* knew how Lily had done it. That made her evening.

It was a great night. It felt like the best Halloween party ever, and all because of the weird mystery at the centre of it. Everyone was saying it was like the old days again, when they were little kids and had got really scared. Sonia Smith told Lily how much she liked her dark purple hair and Sonia's group of clones all agreed with her. "And your *eyes!*" she cooed. "You oughta do them that way – they look twice the size!"

The Parkway Girls kept away from Lily. It was like they knew the night was on her side, not theirs. But Kyle kept close by her.

"You're gonna tell *me*, aren't you, Lily?" he breathed, putting an arm round her. "You're gonna tell me what trick you played?"

"No," she said, "I'm not." But she didn't pull away from him.

She couldn't remember feeling this good, ever.

Chapter 13
Flirting

The good feeling lasted all through the next day. Marsha called round first thing and after she'd sworn to keep it a secret, Lily told her about the crows she'd sort-of tamed in the woods. Then Lily took her down the lane and they found the wings Lily had hidden under the bush.

Marsha thought the whole idea of crow-taming was a bit creepy, but she *loved* the wings. "They're *ace*," she said. "Lily, that is such skill, making them! *God*, I've just had an idea."

"What?" said Lily.

"You know the play the drama group's putting on? It's kind of set in the future, after some disaster has nearly destroyed the earth ... I'm playing a mutant, but a kind of sexy one, kind of a mutant mermaid ..."

"Sounds *fab*," laughed Lily.

"Well, Miss Harland's really stuck on the costumes, she says she's got no idea what to do – Lily, would you come along, and talk to her? You'd be *brilliant*. Wings like this'd be brilliant for the bird mutants. Say *yes*, Lily! Go on – *say yes!!*"

And Lily, of course, said yes. There was nothing better than the feeling of being wanted, it filled you up like good food. Marsha stayed to Sunday lunch. Later, when she'd gone, Tom Morris rang and asked Lily out to see a film that night, but she said no. Everyone knew Tom Morris was a bit of a slag.

Lily was half-hoping Kyle might ring her. But he didn't.

Monday morning was the big test. Lily was trembling inside as she walked tall into school. She'd tossed her new glossy hair back from her face and put on as much eye make-up as Mr Thomas, the head teacher, would allow.

Marsha came up to claim her, and handed her a large black silky scarf that she said was for Lily to keep, "'Cos you look so good in all that Goth stuff."

Sonia Smith and her clones and a few of the other girls all gathered round, chatting and going over the party. They kept on talking about Crow Girl. When they asked Lily how she'd done it, she and Marsha just laughed and ganged up together. Lily said that no magician ever gives away her tricks. And then a few of the boys came over to join them. One of them invited Lily to another party next weekend. And suddenly Lily knew it was OK, it was totally different and OK, as if it had always been as good as this. She knew it wasn't just about looking better though – it was about claiming her space, taking her place. It was about being *her* ...

But the best bit of all was at the end of the school day, when Kyle Hooper came up to her by the school gates – he actually *pushed through three people* to get to her side. "Hey, Lily," he said, "d'you enjoy my party?"

"It was great, thanks," said Lily. "I loved it."

"Glad you did – seeing as you were the star guest!" Then Kyle moved in closer and said, "Come on, Lily! When you gonna tell me how you did that whole Crow Girl thing?"

"You don't give up, do you?" she laughed, with her heart thumping in her chest.

"No. Go on – I won't tell anyone else, I swear."

"OK, I'll tell you."

Kyle grinned.

"I'm the Morrigan," said Lily.

"What?"

"I'm this goddess who turns into a crow to warn people they're gonna die."

"Yeah, yeah," he scoffed.

"*Yeah!* I used to appear on battlefields – I used to scare people stupid!"

"You still do! I nearly broke my neck running when you turned up at the bottom of the garden!"

Then they laughed, really laughed, together. Lily couldn't believe how confident she felt, how ... *powerful*. She wasn't an expert, but this felt like ... the way their eyes were locked together and everything ... this felt like serious flirting! Maybe Kyle was just trying to win her round so she would tell him about Crow Girl, but even so, well ... *why* was he so interested in Crow Girl?

"So are you telling me," said Kyle, "that someone at the party – they're gonna die?"

"Maybe."

"Not me!" He put his hand on her arm, and looked at her, pretending he was terrified. "Tell me it's not me!"

"No! Not you."

"Oh, come *on,* Lily! It was amazing, all those crows and everything ... Tell me how you did it!"

"Oi! Kyle, you tosser!" A football slammed into Kyle's back. Kyle swore and spun round. Three of his mates were standing there, smirking, wanting him to go off with them for a kick-around in the park.

"Better go," he said, all regretful, to Lily. "See you tomorrow, Morrigan!"

"See you!" she said, and started off home.

She was in too much of a state of bliss to see that the Parkway Girls were following her.

Chapter 14
The Chase

"Think you're pretty cool, don't you, Lill – eee?" chanted Tanya.

"Dyeing your hair, slapping stuff round your eyes ..." Jade carried on.

"And all that Crow Girl crap!" Bella added while Jenny sniggered.

Three of the Parkway Girls had a thing about Kyle Hooper. One of them had been out with him, but then been dumped, and two others really fancied him.

And none of the four girls could stand the thought that grotty Lily Stanfield might have a chance with him.

"Think Kyle actually cares about you?"

"Just 'cos he talked to you?"

"He's taking the piss!"

Sick with fear, Lily started to walk faster, but the Parkway Girls walked just as fast. Then she heard one of them hiss, "Come on, *let's get her*!"

Lily had seen how once, last term, they'd held another girl's face down in a muddy puddle and told her she "didn't look so good now". She started to run.

Some instinct made her race for the Wakeless Woods, even though it was the longer way home. What was she doing? There would be far fewer people about and no-one to help her if she got jumped. But

Lily's new fitness was paying off. She ran and stayed quite a bit ahead of them.

The girls didn't like being taken into the wood. "Where we going, freak?" Jade called out.

"*God*, she's weird!"

"You looking for somewhere we can bury you?"

Lily could hear they were nervous. It made her own fear shrink a little. She kept on, deeper into the woods, as the path got narrower and the trees thicker. As she ran, she stuck a hand in her bag, searching for the black, silky scarf Marsha had given her. She found it, pulled it out, and trailed it behind her, a corner in each hand like a cloak.

Or *wings*.

"Oh, *shit*, it's bloody Crow Girl again!"

"You're mad, you know that?"

"Spooky *freak*!"

"Weirdo!"

Even though their shouts were angry, Lily could hear the Parkway Girls were scared. She ran on, into the oval clearing, and stopped dead. Then she turned to face the girls, black scarf flying out behind her.

"Get her!" yelled Tanya – but they'd all stopped.

Lily lifted her arms up, like the Morrigan on the edge of a battlefield warning someone was going to die. Then she let go of the scarf. It swirled up and floated down like a black wraith. It lay on the grass in front of her. Lily made herself stare straight at the four girls, straight into their eyes. Would they dare cross the black scarf?

"Oh, *here* we go," sneered Tanya. "Crow Girl and her stupid party tricks. You might've spooked us at that party, you *freak*, but it won't work here."

"No," squeaked Jade, "for a start, it's not dark."

Lily looked hard at the girls, her eyes fixed on them. "It's *getting* dark, though, isn't it?" she said, in an evil whisper. And she was right – minute-by-minute, dusk was settling eerily on the woods.

"Oh, for *God's* sake – I'm sick of this!" yelled Tanya. She took a step forward.

The others were right behind her, closing in on Lily.

But Lily didn't hesitate. She stepped forward too, right onto the black scarf. She lifted both hands up in the air again. "*Kaa-kaaa-kaaaa*!!" she shrieked.

Shocked, the girls froze.

"*They're coming*!" hissed Lily, right in their faces.

And the crows came!

Four at first, floating down like huge black crosses, then seven, then eleven. The crows flew low, cawing and circling. Lily had no food to give them, but they didn't know that. Lily flung out her arms at the Parkway Girls like a curse, then drew back and flung them out again. In a black cloud of beating wings the crows flew at the heads of the Parkway Girls. They wheeled round and round, beaks and claws thrashing, croaking loud as they searched for Lily's food.

The four girls were terrified. They turned and ran, screaming. They put their arms up in front of their faces, and blundered back along the path that led out of the woods.

And the crows followed them. They swooped at the girls, cawing angrily, soaring from tree to tree and darting down. They were still searching for the food they thought Lily had thrown for them.

Alone in the clearing, Lily sank down onto the ground and hugged herself in relief. "I'm sorry I tricked you, crows," she whispered. "*Oh*, but thank you. *Thank you*!" She could just hear the last few screams of the Parkway Girls as they hurtled out of the woods. She smiled to herself as she thought about how they would stagger home, afraid and humiliated and ... and ... *beaten*.

It was dark now. A thin moon had risen and was shining coldly down into the trees. Lily stood up. She picked up the black scarf, and put it round her shoulders. The crows were beginning to return. One by one they flapped into the clearing and landed on the branches around her. They peered down at her and cawed loudly. "Sorry!" Lily shouted up at them. "Look – it's no good sounding like that, I haven't got any food today! But I will *so* make it up to you tomorrow!" Then she stood quite still and silent, black scarf floating in the wind, as the crows gathered and settled round her in the dark.

Crow Girl! she thought, and a smile lifted her mouth, lit up her whole face. "This isn't just a Halloween trick any more. This is for *real*!"

Barrington Stoke would like to thank all its readers for commenting on the manuscript before publication and in particular:

Joell Anderson

Elizabeth Baguley

Kate Baguley

Stefan Blanchard

Anna Bradshaw

Lauren Brocklehurst

Dee-Dee Broomfield

Kathryn Brown

Helen Charnock

Maria Fitzgerald

Emma-Lauren Green

Colleen Kelly

Jane O'Laughlin

Rosie O'Neill

Kelly Osborne

Mandy Riley

Jessica Shepherd

Bethany Sirl

Shyam Thakrar

Amy Tobin

Tanya Wall

Become a Consultant!

Would you like to give us feedback on our titles before they are published? Contact us at the email address below – we'd love to hear from you!

info@barringtonstoke.co.uk
www.barringtonstoke.co.uk